PEEP SHOW

AN EROTIC ADVENTURE

VICTORIA RUSH

VOLUME 21

JADE'S EROTIC ADVENTURES - BOOK 21

COPYRIGHT

For the uninhibited...

1
———

After going over a week without any type of intimate contact, I was feeling especially horny today. In such circumstances, I'd normally go online to find an outlet to relieve my built-up sexual tension. But lately, I'd been finding that internet porn wasn't doing it for me. Sure, the girls were always hot and sexy and I could generally find something new and interesting to get me in the mood. But it all seemed so impersonal, so *manufactured*. Even my favorite lesbian webcam site had become a disappointment, with viewers swiping from one partner to the next, often right in the middle of a hot-and-heavy session.

I needed some real flesh and blood contact, or at least be able to *see* someone live. But I didn't just want to see and hear her, I wanted to smell her, feel her, *taste* her. Somebody who wouldn't exit the scene at the first sign of boredom, or as soon as she got her rocks off. I wanted to be with someone I could take my time with and enjoy the experience on my own terms. And *Tinder* was out of the question, since I didn't have the time or the energy to vet the candidates, nor string along the ones whose profile never seemed to align with their real personas.

After trolling through the usual online sources, I decided to try something new. I clicked on the latest issue of the Windy City Times, Chicago's long-time LGBTQ newspaper. At least here, I knew I knew I'd be able to find authentic lesbian, bi, and trans girls. Among the litany of gay bar postings, I found an unusual listing in the classified section. Under the headline *Nude Casting Call* was an ad for open auditions at the local theater company. Intrigued, I clicked on the Details tab and began to read the full description:

The Bijou Theater is looking for uninhibited people who are interested in staging solo performances in the nude. With a king-size bed as your primary prop, your goal is to arouse and titillate a live audience using only your body and your wild imagination. There will be boys-only, girls-only, and mixed couples events, so you can cater your performance to your own sexual preference or mix it up as you see fit.

A winner will be chosen after each audition based on audience response, with the winners moving on to regional semi-finals and finals. The Grand Prize winner will win an all-expense-paid vacation for two to the Desire Riviera Maya Resort in Puerto Morales, Mexico. Exhibitionists and voyeurs alike are encouraged to attend. Come one, come all!

Holy shit, I thought, suddenly aware of the growing dampness in my panties. The idea of watching someone perform an erotic routine for a live audience definitely got my motor running. This wasn't some sleazy dive bar or strip club where the girls performed nude dances in front of a bunch of leering men. This was a legitimate theater where amateur performers volunteered to display their naked bodies to a group of of anonymous strangers in a darkened auditorium. And I could *choose* the target audience–no sweaty old men, no creepy lap dances, no private rooms where the girls were paid for private favors. I could just sit back and enjoy the show in the privacy of my own darkened alcove.

But what exactly did they mean by *solo performances*? Just how far did these performances go? Did they touch their bodies only superficially, simulating sex acts like a typical stripper? Or did they caress themselves in their most private regions, with the purpose of genuinely getting themselves and their onlookers off? The presence of a bed on the stage suggested it would be more than just a typical erotic dance. And how much audience participation would there be in the production? Were spectators allowed to actively stimulate *themselves* in the dark while they watched the performers on stage?

The more I thought about it, the more turned on I got imagining how exciting it would be to take in a live performance. Hell, if the conditions were right and the security was good enough, I might be tempted to give it a go myself. But first, I needed to check it out from the protection of the viewing gallery. At least there I'd be able to get my rocks off watching somebody else in the relative safety of a darkened auditorium. We could *both* take our time to ramp up our desire, knowing the only consideration was maximizing everyone's viewing pleasure and satisfaction.

I clicked on the Calendar tab and noticed a selection of dates highlighted in different colors and markings. Pink shading signified ladies-only nights, blue was men-only, and green was open to both sexes. A downward-sloping diagonal line through the box meant the show was sold out for new audience members, and an upward-sloping line meant auditions had been fully booked for that day's event. Scrolling through the pink-shaded boxes, I saw that the next three week's events were X'd out, indicating there was no room for either performers or attendees. The next available ladies night only had one line crossed through it, so I click on the date and booked a ticket immediately.

As I leaned back in my chair, imagining myself watching a pretty girl caressing herself on stage, I pulled down my panties and began rubbing my inflamed clit.

This is going to be interesting, I thought.

<hr>

When the audition night finally arrived, I went to the theater and presented my online ticket to the attendant. A few other girls were waiting along with me behind the turnstiles, and after security checked our driver's licenses to verify our age and sex, they handed each of us a small bag and we entered the darkened theater, locating the closest seats to the stage. I peered in the bag and saw that it contained two items: a disposable plastic seat cover and a small box of Kleenex tissues. I smiled knowingly, then carefully spread the latex cover over the top of my chair. When I sat down and peered around me, I noticed that the room was only half full. Most of the seats were occupied by lone viewers with at least two or three open spaces separating them. I nodded, happy with the way the theater had set everything up for the maximum privacy and comfort of the spectators.

But I noticed there was also a sprinkling of same-sex couples strewn about the theater who were giggling and making out in their private cubbyholes. There was just enough light to notice that everybody was female, but not enough to establish their identities. Suddenly, the lights dimmed and a middle-aged woman walked out onto the middle of the stage under a bright spotlight. I recognized a familiar shape in the shadows behind her, and my heart began to flutter knowing that a nude performer would soon be lying on the bed, giving us a show to remember.

"Good evening, *ladies and voyeurs!*" she announced, holding the mic to her mouth. "Are you ready for some uniquely stimulating entertainment?"

A few people whooped and hollered, while others clapped excitedly. I wondered how many in the audience were 'regulars' who were there mostly to pass judgement on the performances, versus the first-timers like me who were there mostly for the intrigue and the stimulation.

"Those of you who've been here before already know the rules," the woman continued. "But allow me to educate the rest of the crowd to ensure the safety and satisfaction of all participants."

The buzz in the theater suddenly subsided as everyone allowed the MC to finish her briefing.

"Audience members are permitted to encourage the performers with verbal feedback, but we ask that you keep it upbeat at all times. Many of our performers are first-time auditioners, and we wish to provide them with a positive environment to express themselves openly. At the end of each performance we'll ask for your collective feedback to help us judge who should be moved on to the next stage of the competition. No booing or cat-calls–only clapping or cheering to reflect the degree to which you felt entertained. As always, we ask you to remain in your seats until the end of each performance unless you need to use the restrooms in the rear of the theater. For the safety and privacy of every performer, no one will be permitted to approach the stage at any time. Anyone breaking these rules will be promptly escorted out of the theater."

The woman paused for a moment to make sure everyone understood the ground rules. I nodded my head, beginning to appreciate the level of safety and security afforded the performers and audience members alike.

"Any questions?" the MC asked.

The room filled with silence, as everybody anticipated the next move.

"All right then," she said, swinging her arm to the side of the stage where the spotlight focused on a closed curtain hanging in the wings. "Let the show begin!"

As she receded to the opposite side of the stage, the curtain parted and a young woman looking to be in her late teens or early twenties tiptoed out onto the stage wearing a thin bathrobe. She glanced shyly toward the darkened auditorium, then walked purposefully across the stage to the king-size bed, now brightly illuminated under two crisscrossing spotlights. When she reached the edge of the bed, she paused for a moment then pulled her robe off her body and hung it on the side of the headboard, quickly slipping under the linen sheets.

I was able to catch just enough of her naked body to see that she had a petite frame and an agile figure. Her ass was firm and round, and her legs tapered with the grace of a short-track sprinter. I wondered if she might have been a college athlete. Because she'd turned her body away from the audience as she got under the covers, I wasn't able to see much of her upper body, which she'd kept carefully covered with crossed arms. But her face was young and pretty, with the plump skin, full eyebrows, and the unruffled hairstyle of a carefree adolescent.

My pussy twitched as I watched her climb into the bed, pulling the sheets high up under her neck with two hands. I smiled at how shy she was and wondered what had prompted her to participate in such an event if she felt so nervous about displaying her body. Maybe it had been a dare between her and her friends, or maybe her boy or girl-friend had put her up to it, or maybe she just wanted to experience the excitement of being naked in a room full of strangers. Either way, I found the whole premise highly stimulating, and I squirmed in my seat as I found myself getting more turned on by the moment.

I'd decided to wear a mid-length skirt and button-up blouse with no underwear underneath to provide maximum freedom of movement in the event I had the opportunity to touch myself. As I watched the girl lower one hand down the front of her abdomen under the thin sheet, my legs began to spread apart unconsciously. She still held the covers tightly under her chin with one hand, but the flimsy fabric mean-dering like a snake left little doubt what she was doing. At first, she teasingly cupped one of her breasts with her free hand, pinching the nipple with her fingers as her eyes darted tentatively around the darkened theater. I could tell she was nervous and excited at the same time, and I was happy she couldn't see any of our faces to embolden her actions.

Mmm, a few people in the audience hummed, encour-aging her to continue. The girl smiled then inched her hand lower down her abdomen. When it reached the top of her hips, I saw her fingers probe the area near the base of her mound, and her face twitched when she found her sensitive spot. As she began to circle her fingers over her love button, my own fingers began to inch under my skirt toward my tingling gland. There was something incredibly sexy about watching a young girl touch herself under the covers, knowing that everyone's eyes in the room were glued on her.

With the murmurs from the audience turning from hums of approval to gentle moans, the girl slowly began to spread her legs, as the movement of her hand between her legs started to speed up. I could see her chest beginning to rise and fall as her desire began to mount, and she tried to keep a straight face as her lips puckered and her eyelashes batted intermittently while a gentle flush began to spread over her cheeks.

"Show us more!" one of the couples in the corner yelled.

The girl stopped moving for a moment, temporarily taken aback by the intrusion, then she slowly lowered the cover down to the base of her hips. Her tits were small but perky, resting high on her chest in a sexy crescent shape, with large areolas and dark nubs. She lifted her other hand from under the sheet and cupped both of them, pinching her hardening nipples between her fingers.

"*Yes*," somebody purred a few rows in front of me.

Emboldened by the audience's reaction, the girl soon traced one hand back down under the sheets and resumed stimulating her pussy. As I watched the sheets tenting and puffing from the action of her hand, I slipped my own hand under my skirt and began mimicking her movement, stroking and caressing my little man-in-the-boat. I didn't know exactly why, but I found the experience of watching a live girl touching herself in a darkened theater much more arousing than watching somebody masturbate online.

I was dying to see more of her body and just when I was about to encourage her to pull the sheets down a little further, someone else in the audience beat me to it.

"Let us see your pretty pussy," someone called from the back of the theater.

The girl paused for a moment, unsure how much she wanted to reveal. Then she drew her legs back together and pulled the covers down over her knees. I could see her hairy muff sitting on top of her mound, glistening from the juices she'd been spreading over the area with her free hand. She began to separate her legs, then suddenly stopped, not ready to reveal her most private areas to a room full of strangers. But her heaving chest indicated that she was still turned on and desperate to touch herself.

Suddenly, she flipped over onto her stomach, placing both of her hands under her crotch with her legs tightly closed. As I watched her buttocks flexing and her hips pressing rhythmically down onto the mattress, it became apparent to everyone watching exactly what she was doing with her hands. While her hips began to flop up and down on the mattress, her mouth spread open as a flush rolled over her face.

Fuck, I murmured to myself, watching her jill herself under her stomach. *That is so hot!*

Seeing her masturbating so demurely with her pretty ass and back toward us was somehow even more of a turn-on than watching her close-up. I thrust my fingers inside my cunt and began fucking myself more vigorously, imagining myself straddling her with a strap-on dildo.

God, how I'd like a piece of that pretty ass.

"Spread your legs further apart!" someone called from the other side of the theater.

As if on cue, the girl began to spread her thighs until they were separated about thirty degrees apart. I could now see her fingers moving rapidly between her cleft with the underside of her glistening slit poking tantalizingly between her pink globes.

As the sound of impassioned sighs and moans began to spread around the theater, I glanced around me and noticed the telltale sign of movement in the adjacent seats. Many of the girls in my row had their legs spread wide apart as they stroked their pussies while they watched the pretty girl on the stage grow increasingly excited. I glanced at one of the couples in the corner and saw that one girl had her leg raised over the armrest while her partner rammed her fingers into her snatch as she kissed her passionately.

Suddenly, the girl on the stage began to moan more loudly as she angled her ass upwards, spreading her knees further apart. We could now see her entire glistening vulva, highlighted by the twin spotlights shining on her ass, from her pretty pink pucker down past her slit all the way to her hairy muff. As she sped up the movement of her right hand circling her clit, she reached further down between her legs with her other hand and inserted two fingers inside her hole.

She was now unashamedly fucking herself with two hands for the entire theater to see, with no further impediments, or hint of shyness. I could hear the sound of other fingers sloshing in and out of pussies all around me as other horny audience members rammed themselves in sympathy with the girl on the stage. Within seconds, a crimson flush spread over the girl's cheeks and her buttocks began to tremble. As her knees began to wobble from side to side, she squealed like an injured animal, caught up in the throes of a powerful orgasm.

Watching her come in full view of the surrounding audience was more than I could bear, and I arched my back, clamping down hard over my fingers, spraying my pent-up juices all over the metal back of the seat in front of me. As soft gasps and groans emanated from every corner of the theater, the turned-on crowd released their own pent-up pleasure in tandem with the pretty co-ed. I glanced over at the lesbian couple in the corner and saw the girl with her leg over the armrest convulsing in pleasure as her partner rammed her fist into her while they both watched the stage, transfixed by the erotic performance.

When the pretty coed finally stopped shaking, she pulled the sheets back up over her body and the stage darkened, as the spotlight shifted to the curtains on the opposite side of the rostrum. The MC walked back out onto the platform, holding a small device in her hand.

"What did you guys think?" she asked, pointing her smartphone out to the crowd. "Was that worthy of an encore appearance?"

"Woo-hoo!" some audience members hollered.

I noticed a needle swing clockwise on the decibel-reading app.

"Let's give the young lady a *proper* round of applause," the MC hollered. "Show her how much you all *really* enjoyed the performance!"

The crowd erupted in applause and cheering, demonstrating their appreciation and satisfaction with the performance. I noticed the needle swing about sixty percent of the way around the circle, and the MC turned the device around to register the results.

"Let's take a little breather while we give our next performer a few minutes to prepare," she nodded. "But compose yourselves, because the next performer is a crowd favorite!"

As the woman strolled back into the shadows, a group of

stagehands began remaking the now empty bed with a fresh set of linens.

I wish they'd offer us a similar turndown service, I thought as I wiped the back of the seat in front of me with one of the napkins provided in my care package. *Because if that girl only justifies a rating of sixty percent, I'm going to need some fresh towels before this evening is over.*

2

As I watched the next three performers, I grew increasing aroused by the sexually charged atmosphere in the room. At the end of the evening, the prize for best performance was awarded to an older, more seasoned actor, but I couldn't get the image of the young coed shaking quietly on the bed out of my head. There was something about her self-effacing nature that turned me on like no one I'd seen in a long time. I went home that night and had three more powerful orgasms imagining it was *me* planted between her thighs instead of her hand.

But I had far from satisfied my thirst for this intoxicating production. I immediately booked the next available ladies-night audition then spent the next two weeks practicing my own erotic act in front of my full-length dressing mirror. I wasn't quite ready to go on stage and bare my soul for a room full of strangers, but I found the idea incredibly stimulating, and every time I thought about it I came harder than I had in a long time.

When the night of the next auditions rolled around, I

was already soaking wet by the time I entered the building's lobby. I looked around me and saw a familiar collection of singles and couples waiting to be admitted, but there was one pretty girl at the end of the line who caught my eye. Wearing black tights and a loose-fitting, cropped t-shirt, her tight ass and plump breasts barely concealed by her open midriff got me even more excited. As I stole glances at her sexy body, dribbles of lubrication began streaming down the inside of my thighs under my pantyless skirt.

Everybody seemed too nervous to strike up a conversation while we waited to go inside, embarrassed by the obvious reason for our attendance at the event. Like a bunch of perverts in a peep-show theater, we just wanted to hide in the shadows while we silently got our rocks off watching the action on the stage. I turned my body sideways, trying to distract the girl's attention from the river cascading down my legs while pretending to fish around for something in my purse.

After presenting my ID to the security guard, I hurried through the turnstiles and walked into the darkened theater. It was more full than last time, but I found a secluded seat about fifteen rows back from the stage. As the lights began to dim in preparation for the main event, another viewer side-stepped her way into my row and stopped a few seats away from me. I looked up and noticed that it was the girl from the lobby.

"Is this spot taken?" she asked, pointing to the seat next to mine.

I glanced around the theater noticing a few other open spots slightly further back, but for some reason I didn't mind having my personal space encroached upon this time.

"Um, no," I said, motioning to the open seat. "Help yourself."

The girl opened her care package and spread the disposable seat cover over the chair then sat down, placing her purse on the opposite armrest. It felt a bit uncomfortable having someone sitting so close to me, but my rapidly beating heart belied my true feelings.

"It's a little busier than usual tonight," she said, spreading her legs apart to make herself more comfortable.

I glanced down between her thighs and noticed a dark patch in the crotch of her tight pants. Apparently more than one of us had gotten herself worked up in preparation for the night's festivities.

"Oh?" I said, pretending to be disinterested. "I wouldn't know–it's only my second time coming to this event."

"This must be my seventh or eighth time at least" she said, not letting me off the hook so easily. "When were you last here?"

"Two weeks ago, on the last ladies' night."

"I remember that one," she nodded. "That was the one with the cute college girl who needed a little extra encouragement to show her body."

"Yes."

"She was a hot little thing, wasn't she? But I thought she got cheated out the most erotic performance of the night. I guess the more skin they show and the more outrageous the performance, the higher the scores they receive from the hardcore regulars."

"Mmm," I nodded.

"Do you prefer girls?" she asked. "I mean to *watch*?"

"I guess so," I said. "I find them sexier, but I also feel safer around other women. I don't really want to be surrounded by a bunch of lecherous dudes jerking off a few feet away from me."

"I know what you mean," she said, lifting her sneakers off

the floor, one at a time. "At least the theater keeps the place pretty clean. They probably have to send a hazmat team in here after each show."

I shuffled my ass on the latex seat beneath me and smiled.

"Thank heavens for these sanitary seat covers," I said. "I can't imagine sitting anywhere in this place without them."

"And the *napkins*," the girl said, waving one in front of her crotch. "You can never have enough of these things once the action gets hot and heavy."

I was about to introduce myself when the lights in the theater dimmed and the MC walked out onto the stage. But I hardly heard anything she said while I ogled the girl's body next to me. As she leaned back in her seat to get more comfortable, her cutoff shirt slid further up her abdomen, showing the bottom of her fleshy tits. The sensuous curve of her mounds taunted me in the shadows, and I squeezed my thighs together trying to quell my itchy clit.

When I looked back up toward the stage, a sexy blonde girl was kneeling on the bed facing the crowd with her thighs spread about two feet apart. She was wearing a full-length body suit with holes cut out over the tops of her breasts and crotch to reveal her private parts. The effect magnified the size of her breasts, highlighting her pink nipples poking sensuously out of the thin fabric. But it was the effect on her *lower* body than really got my juices flowing. The only part of her crotch that was showing was her bright pink vulva, shining like the petals of a flower surrounded by the darkened landscape of her tight-fitting leotard.

"*Fuck*, that's hot," the girl next to me hissed, spreading her legs wider apart.

The girl on the stage suddenly swung around with her

back to the audience, straightening her legs to her sides as she slowly lowered her crotch to the surface of the bed, performing a perfect split. Then she tilted her ass slightly upward, revealing her pink slit shining like a conch shell on a barren beach. As I squirmed in my chair, mesmerized by the girl's erotic performance, my legs began to spread apart with a mind of their own.

"Do you mind if I make myself more comfortable?" the girl sitting next to me said, pulling her black tights down over her knees. "I'm feeling the need to give my pussy a little breathing room of its own."

"By all means," I said, now fully on board with the idea of having a partner I could enjoy the show with.

She pulled her tights down over her ankles, draping them over the back of the seat next to her, then placed her ankles on the seat rests in front of her, bending her knees as she tilted her hips forward. I could see her bald mound and protruding nub glistening in the reflected light from the stage as my own pussy began to dribble onto the seat cushion beneath me.

Some movement on the stage caught my attention, and I looked up to see the blond girl flip over like a breakdancer, slicing her legs open into a wide scissor shape. With one foot pointed tantalizingly toward the audience and the other nestled under her shoulder, she was practically *begging* us touch her glistening gash.

"*Damn*," my seatmate groaned, now unashamedly rubbing her snatch with her right hand. "I'd sit on that pretty pussy and grind my cunt against hers *any* time."

I slid my hand under my skirt and began to circle my burning nub, thinking exactly the same thing. It had been a while since I'd felt another woman's wet pussy against my own, and I fantasized about kneeling between the blond girl's legs and lowering my hips onto hers.

"Mmm," I nodded as my body began to radiate in pleasure.

Hearing the sound of soft moans and sighs emanating from the amphitheater, the girl suddenly pulled her legs together and pointed them straight up in the air. The curl of her feet and the gentle musculature of her thighs as she flexed her legs reminded me of a ballerina, and I wondered if she might be a professional dancer. But it was the exposed folds of flesh between her tight buttocks that I was focused on at this particular moment. As they spilled out of her torn bodysuit like an open clam shell, my mouth watered imagining myself sucking her pretty pussy while she went through her poses.

Just when I thought it couldn't get any hotter, she lowered her legs into another perfect split framing her face as she peered out into the audience. She began to curl her body forward as she smiled at her hidden admirers while she rolled her fingers over her puffy petals.

"Fuck, yes," the girl next to me hissed, spreading her legs further apart until her knee touched my elbow resting beside her on my armrest. "That is one gorgeous pussy. I'd water that flower any day."

As my seatmate tilted her head back onto the backrest and sped up the motion of her hand between her pussy, the girl on the stage reached under the covers and lifted a strange-looking device into the air above her splayed body. It looked like a type of dildo, but not like anything I'd seen before. This one had deep diagonal grooves in the shaft, making it look like an oversize plastic screw. She tapped a button on the base of the unit it suddenly began to gyrate in a circular flapping motion. Then she held the tip against the opening of her pink slit and slowly sunk the rotating dildo into her hole.

While the crowd watched in mesmerized silence, she began to shake her hips back and forth as she grasped her ankles with outstretched arms. The whole scene looked surreal–like she was some kind of bendable doll with an animatronic dildo flopping around in her snatch as she smiled out into the audience. But the flush spreading across her face quickly reminded me this was no act, as her mouth began to gape open from the pleasure that was spreading inside her body.

Suddenly the girl next to me turned to look for something in her purse and she pulled out a large dildo. I recognized the shape of it instantly, with its penis-shaped tip and protruding rabbit ears on the shaft. She tapped two buttons on the base, then plunged it deep inside her sopping pussy, ramming it in and out of her sloshing hole. Having one just like it at home, I knew exactly what was happening as she held it tightly against her with two hands. While circulating beads around the perimeter of the shaft stimulated the walls of her tunnel, the articulated tip rotated around in circles caressing her G-spot as the flapping external appendages straddled the shaft of her clit, providing intense external stimulation.

As I peered back and forth between the contortionist on the stage and the sexy girl ramming her pussy next to me, I plunged the fingers of my right hand into my hole and began groaning along with the rest of the audience. When the girl on the stage arched her back off the surface of the bed, bringing her face closer to the gyrating instrument flapping wildly inside her pussy, I could feel my own pleasure rising toward its inevitable denouement as my body began to tense up.

Suddenly, her buttocks and thighs began shaking as her head jerked forward and back in unison with the writhing serpent between her legs. I saw her sex flush spread up her long slender neck then all over her face as she grimaced in climactic pleasure.

"Oh my *God*," the girl next to me groaned as her own body began shaking in convulsive spasms with the pulsing vibrator buzzing between her legs. Seeing both girls coming so strongly soon put me over the edge as I slipped my knuckles past the opening to my pussy while I pounded my G-spot with my fist, grunting in a series of powerful contractions.

"Uhn, uhn, uhn," I groaned, feeling the pressure building inside my tunnel.

Just before I finished coming, I pulled my hand out of my hole, jetting my juices forward like a garden hose. The intense spray bounced off the back of the chair in front of me, sprinkling droplets all over the front of my seatmate's body. She looked up at me and mouthed the words *fuck me*, taken aback in surprise. I leaned over and kissed her passionately, cupping her quivering tits as she pressed the still-vibrating dildo hard against her vulva. When we both finally stopped coming, we flopped back against our seat rests, panting in exhaustion from the intense workout we'd both experienced watching the sexy scene on the stage.

3

———

"Holy shit!" the girl next to me sighed when she finally came down from her intense climax. "That was *insane*. I've never seen anything like that before, and I've been to a lot of these performances. Whatever that thing was that was gyrating in her pussy, I want one of those."

"I know what you mean," I said. "I've got a pretty extensive collection of sex toys at home, but I've never seen anything like that before. Watching her use it hands-free with her legs spread apart was incredibly erotic."

As the brightly illuminated bed and the sexy blonde girl receded into the shadows, the MC walked back onto the stage.

"Did you enjoy that performance?" she asked.

"Woo-hoo!" the audience roared in unison.

"Hold up a sec," the MC said, removing her decibel-monitoring app from of her pocket and tapping the screen.

"Now tell me what you *really* think!" she said, turning the device toward the crowd.

Everybody hollered at the top of their lungs, clapping

enthusiastically. The needle swung ninety percent of the way around the arc before stopping near the end of the red zone.

"That's going to be pretty hard to beat," the girl sitting next to me smiled.

She turned and extended her hand over the armrest between us.

"My name's Ashley. I suppose we should introduce ourselves now that we've gotten to know each other a little better."

"Jade," I said, clasping her hand with my wet fingers. "Sorry about the mess–I guess I got a little carried away by that last performance."

"That makes two of us," Ashley said, removing some napkins from her gift bag and handing me a few tissues. "I think you need these more than I do," she said, wiping my juice off the front of her face. "I've never seen a girl squirt as much as you do. You should consider putting on a performance of your own. With your special powers, you'd have a shot at going all the way."

I nodded my head as I cleaned the back of the chair in front of me.

"It's crossed my mind a couple of times. I could sure use a free trip to the tropics. But I'm not sure I've got the nerve to take off all my clothes in front of a group of strangers. I'm enjoying things plenty enough from right here in the viewing gallery."

I watched Ashley remove the dripping dildo from her pussy and wipe it off with a napkin. "What about you? You put on a pretty erotic show yourself. With your hot body, I'm sure you'd get some very appreciative scores of your own."

"I've thought about it," she said. "I guess I just haven't found a strong enough reason to give it a try yet. I'm still thinking of ideas for what I could do that would be new and different."

After the stagehands finished remaking the bed, the MC returned to the stage to introduce the next act.

"That last performance received one of the highest scores in a long time," she said. "But if anyone can top her, I'm guessing this next act has one of the best shots. Prepare yourselves for *Sappho and Aphrodite!*"

The curtain at the side of the stage parted and two naked redheads emerged, walking hand-in-hand toward the bed in the center of the stage. They looked remarkably alike, with similar builds, height, and the same auburn ringlets falling gently over their shoulders. I wondered if they might be twins, and I turned toward Ashley, pinching my eyebrows in surprise.

"I didn't know they allowed tandem acts," I said.

"It happens every now and then," she nodded. "But most people prefer to go solo. It's hard to judge a tandem act in terms of who should move forward to the next round. Sometimes, the MC asks the crowd to rate each performer separately, but in this case these girls almost look like *clones* of one another. It would be impossible to differentiate the two when it comes time to evaluate their performance."

"Do you think they're *sisters*?" I said.

"I dunno, but if they are, that's just notched it up a couple of levels in my books. Let's see how far they take it."

As I ogled the figures of the two girls walking across the stage, my pussy twitched imagining them touching one another. Their skin shone like alabaster under the bright light of the overhead spotlight, their pink nipples glowing like beacons on the pale canvas of their bodies. Their tits were very small, making them almost look like adolescent boys with their flat chests and narrow hips. But when they reached the side of the bed and climbed onto the mattress, their curvy asses and sexy slits left little doubt as to their real sex.

"Mmm," Ashley purred, placing her feet on the armrests in front of her, spreading her thighs apart. "There's nothing like fresh girl meat to get me in the mood. *Two* helpings are making me twice as hungry."

My own pussy pulsed imagining them growing up together, playing in the privacy of their own rooms. Whether they were real sisters or it was just part of their act, I'd already bought into the theme as my juices began to trickle down under my ass.

"They're fucking hot, that's for sure," I nodded, hiking my skirt up to reveal my glistening mound.

"Damn girl," Ashley grunted. "You look pretty edible yourself. I might need to take you home once the show is over to have you for dessert."

"That can be arranged," I purred, giving her a playful wink.

When we turned our attention back to the stage, the girls were lying down beside each other, rubbing their bodies together as they kissed passionately on the bed.

"Something tells me this isn't the *first* time they've been together this way," Ashley mused.

"No," I nodded, my eyes glued on the stage. "I have a feeling they've had quite a few years to prepare for this moment."

As they intertwined their legs and began to grind their mounds together, Ashley and I began to circle our tingling clits with our right hands.

"Mmm," I moaned. "I'd love to feel their sweet bodies pressed up against mine right about now."

"Do you need a little *assist*?" Ashley said, raising an

eyebrow and reaching over the armrest to slip her fingers under my blouse.

"*Fuck*, yes," I hissed, dying to feel someone else's hands on my body.

I spread my legs far apart and rested the underside of my knees over the adjacent armrests like the couple I'd seen at the previous show. Ashley took one look at my pink nub poking its head out of its sheath and placed her other palm over my pussy, caressing my folds with the tips of her fingers.

"Yes, baby," I groaned. "Play with my clit while I watch these cute girls. I want to imagine I'm right there in the thick of the action."

"You like flat-chested girls, do you?" she purred, lifting her fingers to circle my burning jewel.

"Yes," I panted. "I reminds me of my adolescent years."

"Mmm," Ashley mewed. "The great taboo. It's off limits now that we're grown up, but I remember experimenting when I was younger too. I bet those two have been playing with each other for a long time."

"Yes," I groaned, beginning to lose myself in the fantasy.

The two redheads suddenly separated and shifted into a scissor position, lying on their sides as they reached out and clasped hands.

"*Fuck me*," I groaned, watching the two girls rubbing their pussies together.

"Does that turn you on?" Ashley purred, slipping her fingers inside me as she trilled my clit with her thumb.

"You have *no* idea," I purred.

"Oh, I've got a pretty good idea judging by how wet you are," she said. "Are you going to squirt all over their pretty little tits?"

"Fuck yes," I groaned, getting more and more worked up watching the two girls tribbing their wet pussies together.

"What exactly would you do with them if you had the opportunity?" Ashley asked. "What did you use to do with your girlfriends during sleepovers?"

"I'd touch them in their private areas," I panted. "Kiss them, suck them, *probe* them."

Ashley peered at me with a sly smile.

"Trib them, mount them, grind your pussies together?"

"Yes," I groaned, reflecting back on my earliest sexual discoveries.

"Did you squirt back then too?" she asked.

"Not right away. Not until I went through puberty and began lubricating more heavily."

"Did you cum with your little friends?"

"Yes," I said, beginning to tremble from the imagery of the two girls scissoring on the stage, reminding me of my explorative youth.

"What else did you like to do with your pretty girl-friends?" Ashley said, using the show on the stage as a metaphor for reliving my childhood memories.

"Sometimes we'd play with toys..." I said.

As if on cue, one of the girls lifted a long green object from under the covers, placing it between their pussies.

A cucumber! I murmured, remembering the moment when my girlfriends and I discovered how much fun it was to probe our pussies with whatever phallic-shaped objects we could find. As the girls separated their bodies, placing the ends of the cucumber against each of their openings, my juices began pouring over Ashley's hands.

"Do you want me to place my little toy inside you while you channel fucking these girls?" Ashley said.

"Yes, please," I begged, desperate to feel my pussy filled up while I imagined fucking the cute redheads.

Ashley reached over and lifted her rabbit vibrator off her seat cushion and without even bothering to turn it on, she rammed it inside my pussy, beginning to fuck me with the dildo as she leaned over to kiss me. I turned my face toward her and moaned into her mouth as I peered at the spectacle on the stage out of the corner of my eyes. The two girls now had the double-sided dildo deeply embedded in each of their pussies as they ground their vulvas together, moaning in unison. I could see their arms beginning to tense up as they held each other tightly, while their passion slowly built toward a peak.

Ashley tapped the base of the rabbit dildo, activating the dual vibration functions, and I slid down in my seat, pressing the flapping rabbit ears against my pussy.

"Oh *God*, Ashley," I panted. "I'm going to cum baby. I'm going to cum so *hard*..."

As I watched the pre-orgasmic rash begin to spread over the chests of the two pale-skinned girls writhing together on the bed, my pleasure suddenly crested and I groaned a deep guttural growl. As the redheads began convulsing and wailing in union, the walls of my pussy clenched in powerful convulsions and I sprayed my juices out my plugged hole, ricocheting off the top of the vibrator towards Ashley's face.

While I thrashed in my seat squealing in ecstasy, she smiled at me, blinking her eyes between the sprays bouncing off her face while she held the vibrating dildo firmly against my vulva. Suddenly I became aware of similar noises in the theater as other viewers groaned in unison with the two girls shaking on the bed. The action of the two youthful-looking girls had brought back a flood of fond memories and it took a long time for me to stop coming as I watched them pleasure each other on the stage. When I finally came down from my high and collapsed back against my seat, Ashley looked over at me and smiled.

"We've *got* to get together soon," she mewed, lifting her dripping hand to my breast and pinching my erect nipple.

"Let's get out of here," I said, thrusting my tongue into her mouth. "I can't wait a moment longer."

"What about the rest of the show?" Ashley said, motioning to the MC walking back out onto the stage.

"*Fuck* the rest of the show," I said. "Let's make our *own* show. I need to feel your body next to mine before I go crazy."

Ashley paused for a moment, then peered at me with a sly grin. She raised herself out of her chair and sat her naked ass down over my still-fluttering pussy.

"Why wait any longer?" she said, tilting her pussy towards mine as she rested her arms on the seat rest in front of us. "Maybe we can have it *both* ways."

As she began to rock her hips against mine, I felt our clits merge as a new surge of energy rocketed through me. I grabbed her ass with both hands and pulled her closer toward me.

"Fuck yes," I purred. "Let's show these guys how it's really done..."

4

———

After the show, Ashley and I went back to my place and made love all night long. Both of us had ideas for what we'd like to do for our own auditions, and we experimented with different positions and pairings for many hours. By the time I fell asleep at three a.m., I dreamed of all the adventurous things we might try on stage. In the morning, I slipped on a robe and went downstairs to cook up some breakfast and Ashley followed soon after.

"Mmm–that smells good," Ashley said, smelling the bacon and eggs frying in the pan.

"I thought you might be hungry after our little workout last night," I winked.

"*Little*?" she said, raising her eyebrows. "Between the two of us, we must have burned enough calories to light a small city."

I handed her a steaming mug of coffee and sat down on the bar stool next to her.

"That was pretty wild, wasn't it?"

"Are you referring to the action on the stage or how quickly we landed in each other's laps?"

"Both," I smiled. "I don't think I've come so hard as when you were grinding your pussy against mine while we watched the show together in the darkness."

"Viewing a live sex act can be pretty damn stimulating ," Ashley nodded. "I think it's genius what they've created there. I didn't realize how much I enjoyed being a voyeur until I discovered this production. But I think I'm just about ready to flip things around."

"Oh?" I said, lifting the food out of the skillet and placing it on her plate. "You think you're daring enough to bare everything in front of a group of strangers?"

"They won't *all* be strangers," she smiled, caressing my arm with the back of her hand. "*You'll* be there, right? It'll be that much more of a turn-on knowing you'll be watching too."

She paused for a moment as she wolfed down another spoonful of scrambled eggs.

"But it'll be even *more* exciting if we do it together."

"You mean as a tandem act, or each of us separately?"

"Both. It will be exciting for us to perform solo, but we can step it up to the next level if we decide to get together. That way, at least *one* of us will have a chance to win the trip to Mexico."

"You're just hedging your bets in case I win it for myself," I said, crunching on a piece of bacon.

"Well, if we each perform solo, we double our chances. Will you be my plus-one if I win?"

"Or you can be *mine* when *I* win," I smiled.

"Then when we get together as a couple, we can wow the crowd all over again," Ashley said. "It can only *help*, right?"

"I think you might be onto something," I nodded,

finishing the last of my breakfast. "But now I've worked up a whole different kind of appetite. Do you feel like going back upstairs and working on some of our routines?"

"I thought you'd never ask," Ashley said, sliding her last piece of bacon sensuously between her lips.

For the next couple of hours, Ashley and I bounced ideas back and forth as we play-acted our routines in front of one another, giving each other tips and encouragement for how we could ramp up the excitement level. Then we practiced every combination we could imagine for joining together while we watched ourselves in my dressing mirror. By the time we both fell asleep exhausted again, I felt I'd vastly improved my repertoire of girl-on-girl sex.

When the date for the next auditions rolled around, we tingled in excitement waiting in the wings for our turns to go on stage. The first performer was a pretty brunette dressed in a cowboy hat and pantless chaps. She carried a pommel-horse-shaped apparatus onto the stage, then placed it in the center of the bed and plugged it into the nearest power outlet. After screwing a diamond-shaped dildo into the middle of the saddle, she spent the next thirty minutes riding it like a bucking bronco, flailing her arms in the air as the plug vibrated inside her. By the time she'd finished riding it in the forward- and backward-cowgirl positions, Ashley and I estimated that she'd had least four orgasms.

The next performers were a tandem act, dressed in sexy superhero costumes. The lower half of the Batgirl character's costume had been entirely cut away, with her naked ass and bare legs posing a sexy counterpoint to her well-camouflaged upper body covered with a black mask, tight rubber bodice, and flapping yellow cape. Her Catwoman sidekick had the front of her full-length bodysuit slit open down the front, pressing her large round breasts into a sexy cleavage exposed on the front of her chest. They'd had some additional props placed on the stage and the Catwoman character entered first, creeping furtively toward a nightstand at the side of the bed. She opened the drawer, peering nervously around her, then she tucked a jewelry box under her arm.

Suddenly, Batgirl entered from the other side of the stage and confronted the would-be burglar, placing her hands on her hips and shaking her head in disapproval. Catwoman pulled out a whip and snapped it toward her adversary, but the Batgirl used her quick reflexes to sidestep the rippling cord. Then she pulled a foam boomerang out of her utility belt and flung it at Catwoman, striking her in the head as she fell to the floor, pretending to be unconscious. She then carried the girl to the bed and tied her to the four bedposts using wrist ties from her utility belt, spreading her arms and legs in a wide V-shape.

It was only then that I noticed the crotch of Catwoman's tights had also been split open, revealing her pink vulva surrounded by the black bodysuit. As she woke up from her stupor and took stock of her predicament, she sneered at Batgirl, flailing her body helplessly against her binds. Batgirl simply smiled back at her and reached into her utility belt, pulling out a large penis-shaped vibrator. She flipped a button on the base and the dildo began buzzing and throbbing loudly. As Batgirl lowered it toward her captive's open crotch in a threatening gesture, Catwoman thrashed her body on the bed, pretending to be frightened.

The whole scene was over-the-top campy, but somehow

the appearance of the two skimpily clad superheroes pretending to battle created a highly arousing effect. Ashley and I looked at one another shaking our heads in dismay, wondering the same thing.

"I didn't know we were allowed to wear *costumes* and use *props*," she said. "Do you think our act is going to be interesting enough after this performance?"

"Let's see what else they've got in their bag of tricks," I said. "Remember it's not about the size of your package, it's how well you can use it."

As we peered back out onto the stage, Batgirl placed the vibrating tip of the dildo against Catwoman's mound and she suddenly stopped flailing as she lifted her hips to press the device firmer against her vulva. Batgirl peered at her devilishly, then pulled the vibrator away from her pussy as Catwoman feigned frustration. Then she held it against her flapping thighs for a few more seconds before yanking it away once again. They continued this cat-and-mouse routine for a few minutes until Catwoman shook her body angrily, looking at Batgirl with pleading eyes.

Batgirl picked the jewelry case up off the floor and pointed toward it with a disapproving stare, then motioned toward the nightstand where it belonged. Catwoman nodded her head in acquiescence, then Batgirl placed the container back in the table and held the vibrator high up in the air for the audience to see. They cheered her loudly, encouraging her to place it back on Catwoman's twitching vulva. But this time she inserted the huge phallus into Catwoman's pussy until it was fully embedded inside her. Then she proceeded to pump it in and out of her hole as Catwoman became increasingly aroused, moaning and writhing on the mattress until she climaxed in a powerful orgasm. When they finished their routine, the audience roared in approval, clapping enthusiastically.

"That's gonna be pretty hard to beat," Ashley said, knowing it was her turn to go on next. "Maybe I should have dressed up in a costume or brought some extra props."

"Don't worry about what other people are doing," I assured her, squeezing her hand gently. "With your hot bod and your sexy routine, you'll have them eating out of your hands in no time."

"Or hopefully my *crotch*," she smiled at me nervously.

"Exactly," I said. "Go do your thing. Remember, I'll be here watching the whole time getting turned-on along with you."

"Mmm," Ashley purred. "That'll help. Maybe I won't need as much lube after all."

I smiled back at her, nudging her out the curtain, and she walked toward the newly remade bed with her hands resting in the side pockets of her robe. We'd both agreed that her act would be sexier if she revealed her body in stages, teasing the audience about what she intended to do on stage. When she reached the bed, she climbed up onto the mattress and straddled the brass headboard, placing one knee on the pillow and her other foot on the opposite rail for support.

She began rocking her hips sexily on the top rail and opened the front of her robe, showing her plump tits sitting high on her chest. As she slowly slid her body toward the corner bedpost, she peered up at me and I nodded, circling my hand over my crotch to signal how much her act was turning me on. When she reached the end of the rail, she grasped the small brass globe topping the post and rolled her hands over it like she was giving it a sexy hand job. But she and I both knew she was actually lubing the ball with some tissues she'd hidden in her pockets. Then she lifted herself up and straddled the post between her thighs, lowering herself down a few inches.

To the audience watching from an oblique angle, they couldn't have known immediately what she was doing, with her robe still covering half of her body. But for me watching directly in front of her, I could see that she'd embedded the brass finial deep inside her pussy. When she reached back and pulled her robe off her body, an audible gasp rose from the audience when they finally realized what she was doing. With appreciate applause wafting up from the seats, Ashley placed both of her hands on the top rail and began to rock her body up and down over the brass bulb. As it became obvious she was fucking the bedpost, many observers began to moan while they stimulated themselves watching her erotic act.

When she peered back over towards me, I was squeezing my right breast tightly while my other hand fluttered between my legs. I nodded at her quietly as my body began to tremble in concert with hers, losing myself in her performance. Even though we'd talked about what we planned to do once we were on stage, I hadn't realized how sexy it would be to watch her first hand with the audience buzzing around us.

As Ashley became increasingly aroused listening to the reaction of the audience, she turned her body to face them directly, spreading her knees wide apart so they could clearly see her impaled over the bedpost. Her movements began to pick up in intensity and her neck muscles started to tighten as she approached climax. Suddenly she lurched forward, jerking her body forward and back from the convulsions racking her body.

As I watched her shaking in the throes of agony, I came

unconsciously watching my new friend pleasure herself in front of the large audience. After many long seconds of quivering in pleasure, she slowly lifted herself off the glistening pole and pulled her robe back over her body, scampering off the stage in my direction. As the lights fell over the platform, the audience cheered loudly in appreciation of her sexy and original performance.

5

———

"What did you think?" Ashley said, scurrying up next to me.

"That was fucking hot," I said, holding her tightly as I motioned toward the still-buzzing amphitheater. "And judging by the audience reaction, *they* enjoyed it too. How did it feel being on stage? Were you nervous at all?"

"A little at first," she nodded. "But once I got that ball inside me, I wasn't thinking of much else. Other than watching *you,* of course. Knowing you were getting turned on watching me was more exciting than knowing everybody else was watching me."

"I'm glad," I said. "Did you enjoy yourself?"

"You have no idea," she smiled. "Let's just say the turnaround crew might need a little longer to clean up the bed in preparation for the next act.

"Speaking of which," she said, slipping her hand inside my robe to cup my quivering breast. "Are you ready to go out there? You seem a bit nervous yourself."

"That's just me still feeling excited from watching you.

I've never felt more ready to do something like this in my whole life."

"Break a leg, babe," Ashley smiled. "Just make sure you don't break anything *else*." She held up her hands as I turned around for her to help me disrobe. "Are you sure you want to go out there completely naked?"

"It'll just get in the way," I said. "I just want it to be my naked body they're focused on. Hopefully that'll be enough."

"You don't need any props or extra embellishments," Ashley said. "You'll be doing something nobody's ever seen before."

"Wish me luck then," I said, hearing the MC come back out onto the stage to introduce the next act.

"You won't need it," Ashley said. "I'll see you soon."

I smiled back at her, knowing it would be sooner than anybody expected.

As the MC motioned toward the stagehands, the curtain swung open and I strutted across the stage, relishing every step as the audience took in my taut, hourglass figure. I'd worked hard to keep my thirty-something body in good shape and as I extended my legs with each step, wiggling my ass and holding my chest high, my body surged with fire. I was about to do something I'd never tried before, and the idea of touching myself in front of a room full of strangers electrified me.

When I reached the bed, I lay down on it face up and reached behind me to grasp the headrail with both hands. I could still feel traces of Ashley's lubrication on the bar, and it excited me as I pulled my legs up and over my head, showing the crowd my bald pussy and ass. A few girls hollered their approval, and I spread my legs into a wide 'V' so they could see my glistening bald pussy more easily. A few people applauded my limber body, but after the previous week's sexy contortionist act, I knew they were looking for something more.

I caressed the insides of my thighs, stopping tantalizingly short of my pink folds, then turned around and placed my hips against the headboard, tilting my head as I peered at the audience upside down. They cheered loudly at my taunting gesture, knowing it was just a warm-up for the main act. Then I lifted my legs straight up above my body and slowly lowered them backwards toward my head. I'd been working on my flexibility in the weeks leading up to the performance and didn't have any difficulty resting my toes on the surface of the bed a few feet behind my head.

At this point all the audience could see was the slit of my ass with my face concealed by my closed legs. As they continued to cheer me on, I began to spread my feet apart until my legs were separated about sixty degrees. I could have easily spread them further apart, but that wasn't the main purpose of my routine. I placed the palms of my hands over each of my buttock cheeks and pulled my hips further down, moving my dripping pussy closer to my face.

With my toes inching further down toward the foot of the bed, the audience slowly began to realize what I was trying to do. As a loud murmur spread across the auditorium, I watched my slit move ever-closer to my puckering lips. With my erect clit quivering only inches from my mouth, I tilted my head back and peered toward the audience again, licking my lips in anticipation.

Realizing I was only inches away from taking my glistening gland into my mouth, their cheers grew in increasingly loud as I pressed my feet further down the mattress, lowering my box closer to my waiting mouth. Even though I'd practiced this hundreds of times before, knowing that so many eyes were watching me from the darkened auditorium raised my excitement to a whole new level. As my juices poured out of my slit over the top of my mound, I pulled my hips forward with one last tug, enveloping my hot gland with my moist lips.

A loud gasp suddenly arose from the audience, who'd never expected me to accomplish this feat of gymnastic elasticity. As I began to circle my tongue around my bright red jewel, a series of loud moans emanated from every corner of the auditorium. The crowd's reaction to my unique form of self-stimulation only increased my excitement as I lowered my hips even further, stroking my glistening slit up and down with my outstretched tongue. It was obvious that no one in the audience had ever seen anyone do anything remotely like this before, and I smiled as I listened to their shocked reaction.

As I licked the sides of my labia, pausing for long moments to suck my erect clit, I spread my legs further apart so they could see my pink pucker shining between my ass cheeks. I was putting every part of me out there for display, and the eroticism of the act lifted my passion with every passing moment. As I began to feel my pleasure rising toward its inevitable peak, I turned my face toward Ashley watching from the wings, and I nodded my head gently.

We'd both choreographed this routine carefully, and it was *her* I really wanted to cum with, not just the audience. Ashley dropped her robe on the floor and began walking onto the stage in my direction. When the audience saw that I'd enlisted an accomplice into my sexy act, their cheer rose even louder.

When Ashley reached the edge of my bed, she positioned herself behind my hips, peering down into my splayed, glistening slit. She smiled sexily at me, then grabbed one of her tits and leaned forward, stroking it against my wet opening. As she slid it toward my quivering mound, I popped my clit out of my mouth and began sucking on her nipple, alternating between her erect nub and mine. As the groans from the appreciative audience grew louder and louder, we smiled at each other, knowing we'd created something new and memorable.

But we were far from finished titillating the crowd, and I was still aching to come. I'd been holding back my orgasm until she joined me on the bed and as she peered into my glassy eyes, she pulled her body back until her face nestled directly between my thighs. While I resumed sucking my burning glans, she slowly licked my slit downward until she reached my pink rosebud. Without pausing for a second, she began circling my pucker with her long outstretched tongue, as my face began to turn redder and redder in mounting ecstasy.

As I felt my orgasm begin to wash over me, we locked eyes and I grunted loudly as my pussy began to clench in powerful contractions. I squirted my pent-up juices out of my pussy all over Ashley's pretty face embedded between my quivering cheeks. With my lips locked over my twitching clit and my entire body convulsing on the bed, I watched the muscles on the underside of my vulva pulsing as I sprayed squirt after squirt over Ashley's face mere inches in front of me.

The theater was now awash in the sounds of simultaneous orgasms as girls jilled themselves excitedly watching the two of us joined together in one of the sexiest routines they'd ever witnessed. Ashley reached between her legs and moaned into my crevasse as she popped off with the rest of the crowd. By the time I'd finished spraying her face and my clit stopped pulsing in my mouth, she leaned forward and kissed me passionately between my legs. As we lay there together for a long moment reveling in the reaction of the crowd, we nodded toward each other knowing we'd created a once-in-a-lifetime performance.

But we still had one ace up our sleeves to guarantee that at least one of us would be moving forward in the competition. With a sly grin, Ashley raised herself off the bed and straddled her feet between my hips as she peered down at my dripping crotch. Then she slowly squatted her body down until her ass cheeks rested against mine. I pulled my legs forward a few inches and bent my knees, tilting my hips backwards her until our pussies touched.

As we began to rock our bodies together, I watched her labia twisting and stretching against mine while we moaned in delirious pleasure. I was already buzzing from my last orgasm, and as we angled our hips toward one another, our clits touched and we gasped when we felt our sensitive organs melding together. As her slippery ass slid effortlessly over mine from our combined juices still coating our bodies, she reached down to hold my hands. I intertwined my fingers with hers as I peered into her eyes, feeling another powerful orgasm beginning to overtake me.

The feeling of her erect clit rolling over mine as our asses rubbed together was sublime. Although we'd experimented with the routine in the days leading up to this week's performance, there was something about the audacity of performing it live in front of a crowd of strangers that raised the excitement level even higher for both of us. As Ashley's mouth began to spread open while she approached another powerful orgasm, she peered down at me and mouthed the words *I love you*. By now, neither of us were paying any attention to the moans and groans emanating from the audience as we gripped each other's hands tightly while our pleasure consumed us.

Suddenly, Ashley let out a howl as her body began convulsing overtop of my hips. Watching her come with her pussy joined together with mine quickly put me over the edge also as I began spraying out in every direction from the tight seal between us. While I watched the spectacle from my prone position with my juices splashing all over our tits and faces, I saw my rosebud clamping rhythmically inches from my face. When we both finally finished shaking in a uniform mash of merged flesh, Ashley dropped down onto the bed beside me and kissed me gently.

"If *that* doesn't get us a free trip to the Desire resort in Mexico," she panted, "I don't know what will."

I peered over toward her and smiled.

"Who needs a trip to Mexico when we've got all the stimulation we need right here?"

Everybody's an exhibitionist in disguise...

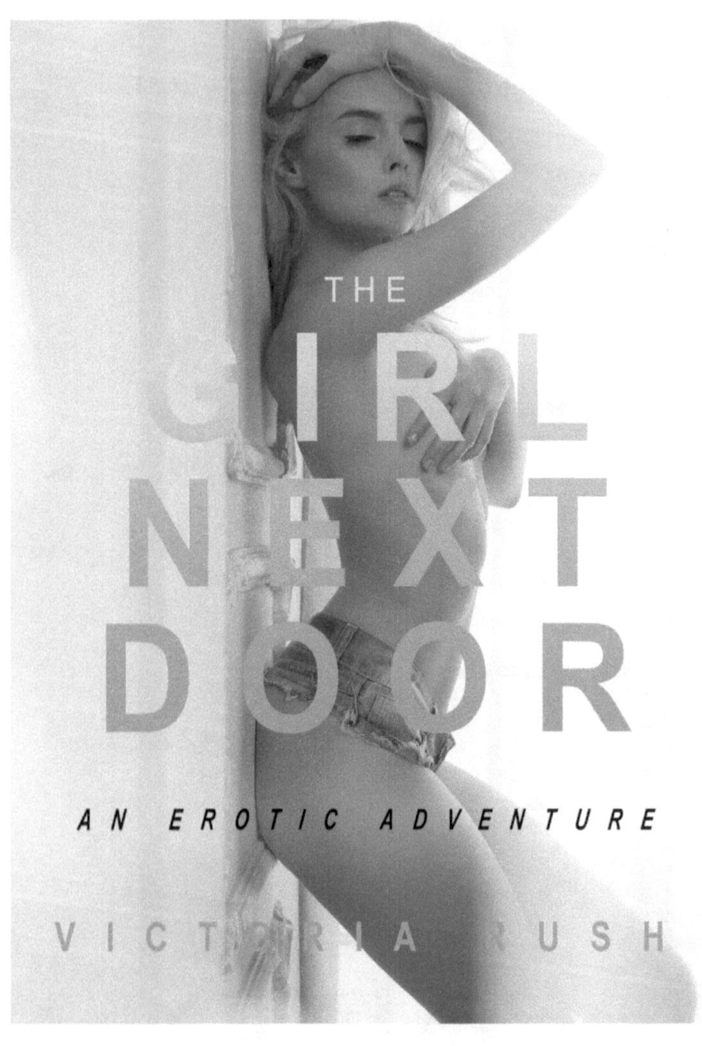

Spying on the neighbors just got a lot more interesting...

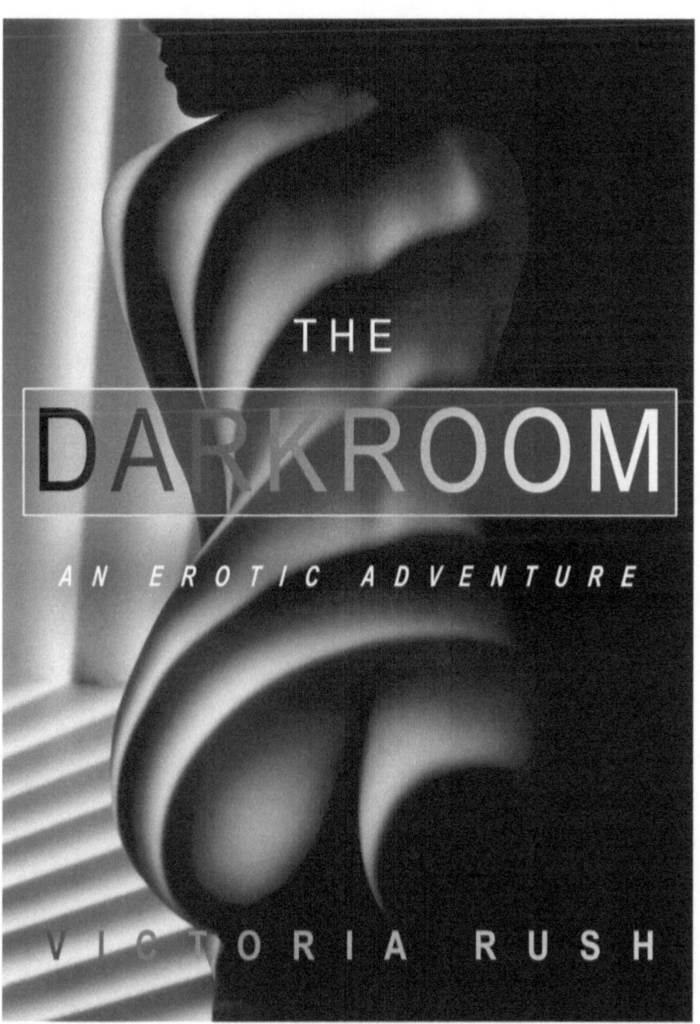

Everything's sexier in the dark...

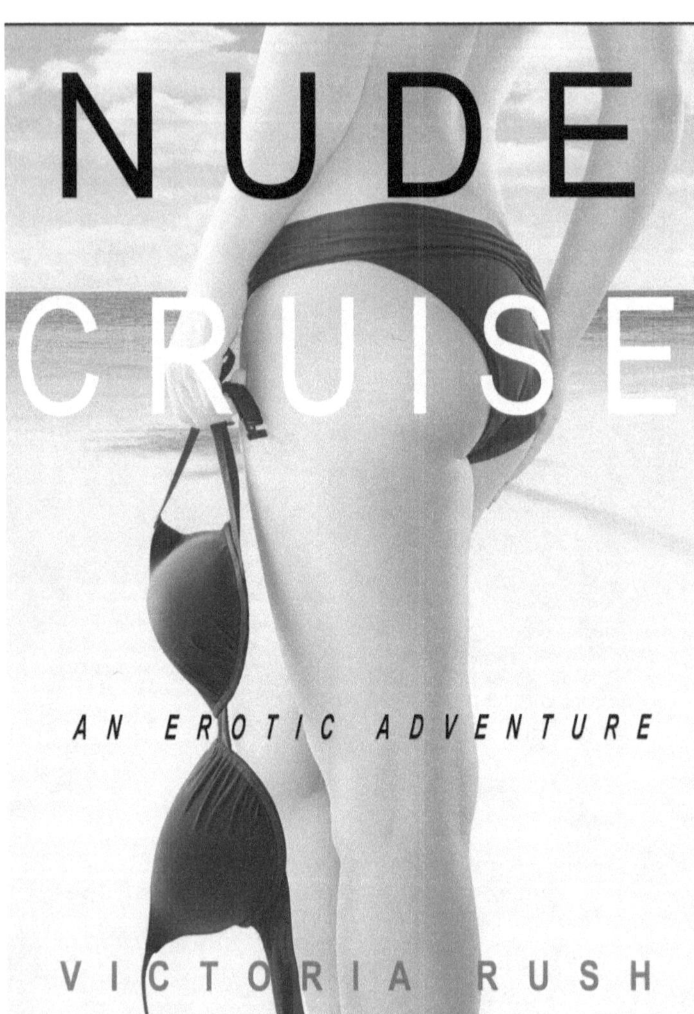

Some people get wet on a cruise for different reasons...

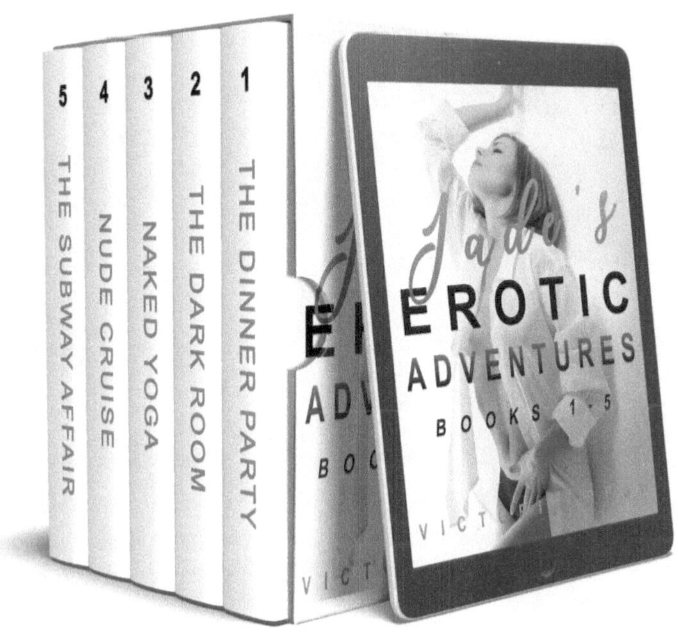

Books 1 -5 in the bestselling series - 60% off

THE DINNER PARTY - PREVIEW

FINGER FOOD

Sometime later, I heard a soft tap on my bedroom door. Not wanting to remove myself just yet from my cocoon of luxury, I called out to answer.

"Yes?"

"It's time for your massage," a woman's voice replied.

"Just one minute please."

I reluctantly stepped out of the bath and quickly toweled myself dry. I wrapped a large bath sheet around me, re-donned my mask, then opened the bedroom door.

A petite young Asian girl greeted me, wearing a kimono similar to mine and a crimson masquerade mask.

Apparently not everybody who works here always walks around stark naked.

The girl was utterly breathtaking. Long jet-black hair cascaded over high cheekbones past pouty lips, her delicate collarbones peeking from the top of her kimono. I could see her breasts and hips outlined by the tightly-wrapped kimono and suddenly wished that she too had come to my boudoir naked.

"My name is Jasmine," she said. "I'm your personal

masseuse and esthetician. Are you ready for your final preparation?

Just the thought of this beauty laying her tender hands on me sent a shiver down my spine.

"Definitely. Please come in. How would you like me to prepare?"

"Come with me, please."

Jasmine led me into the bathroom, where she nonchalantly removed her kimono and hung it behind the bathroom door.

Oh my God.

I didn't think anyone in this place could get more beautiful or sensuous. Jasmine had perfectly shaped B-cup breasts with a thin indentation running down the center of her perfectly toned stomach. Like everyone else in this place, her pubis was utterly bald and flawless. She barely looked eighteen and I was just about to ask her age, but she spoke first.

"If you'd like to remove your towel and lay face down on the table, we can get started. May I call you Jade?"

There was something about her confident manner and tone that belied her youthful appearance. I had no inhibitions whatsoever about displaying myself unclothed to this stranger.

"Yes, thank you, Jasmine." I unhooked my bath sheet and threw it against the side of the tub.

"Would you like me to drape your backside?" Jasmine asked.

"That won't be necessary," I quickly answered.

Jasmine walked over to the vanity counter and picked up two small bottles of oil resting under an orange radiant lamp. She brought them back to the massage table, opened one, and poured the oil into one cupped hand then rubbed her hands together. The scent of lavender wafted toward my nose.

I closed my eyes in anticipation of her touch. I'd had massages before, but nothing as sensuous and stimulating as this. When her hands touched the small of my back, I jerked reflexively from the sexual tension. My heart was beating a hundred miles an hour as I felt the blood coursing through my veins.

Jasmine must have sensed my nervous tension and began pressing her fingers more firmly into my back as she moved them slowly up each side of my spine. The warm oil allowed her hands to glide effortlessly across my skin. She used every surface of her hands to massage my muscles, expertly kneading my skin with her fingers and palm.

I began to relax as my muscles softened and surrendered to her touch. She sensuously massaged every part of my back, shoulders, and neck, applying just the right amount of pressure. Periodically, she would pour more warm oil on my lower back, dipping her hands in it to replenish the silky lubrication against my pliant skin.

Just as the sexual tension began to subside from the utter relaxation of the massage, Jasmine moved her hands down to my buttocks and began to caress them in soft circular motions. My glutes contracted involuntarily and I unconsciously pressed my mound into the firm padding of the table. Suddenly I was quickly reminded that a gorgeous young woman was caressing my naked body. She cupped each buttock between her hands as she massaged my ass tantalizingly, her little finger sliding slowly into the cleft just above my anus.

Periodically, I'd partially open one of my eyes with my head turned in her direction to look at her gorgeous body. My head was at the same level as her midsection, and my mouth watered as I watched her stomach muscles flex and her hips undulate with each movement of her hands. At times her pussy was almost right beside me and I wanted to reach out and run my own fingers up her soft legs.

I was in total heaven and getting wetter by the moment. Just when I thought I couldn't stand it anymore, she suddenly moved her hands down to my feet and began massaging her thumbs into my soles.

I'd always loved having my feet massaged, but nobody did it like Jasmine. She cradled my foot and used every part of her hands to massage and knead every surface from my heel to my toes. I didn't want her to stop, but there were other parts of my body that were screaming for attention.

As if reading my thoughts, she began moving her hands up toward my calf, using her thumbs to spread the muscle apart. She lingered almost as long on my calf as she had on my foot, rolling the ball of my calf between both of her hands, sliding her slick hands up and down erotically. I couldn't help imagining how she might use those same hands to massage a man's erect cock in a similar manner. My mind wandered again to what pleasures lay in wait for me over dinner.

After shifting her hands to my right leg and giving my other foot and calf similar attention, she placed each hand just behind my knees and began to slowly move them up towards my buttocks. Her thumbs pressed against my inner thighs as she glided tantalizingly close to my apex.

I rolled my legs outward in an invitation to move closer. My legs were parted enough that I was sure she could see my vulva from her vantage point behind me. In my highly aroused state, my lips were engorged and spread apart, revealing my moist and quivering opening.

But as much as I desperately wanted her to, Jasmine

never touched me there. She repeatedly slid her hands right up to the edge of my slit, pressing and rotating her thumbs on the fleshy meat of my upper thighs just below my aching pussy. I suppose this was part of her master plan—to tease me mercilessly and inflame my passions so I'd be ready for just about anything at the main event.

It was certainly working. After thirty minutes of Jasmine's ministrations, I was grinding my pussy into the table trying desperately to give my clit some needed direct stimulation.

Just when I thought I couldn't be teased any more tantalizingly, Jasmine opened one of the bottles of warm oil and poured it directly into the crack of my ass. She paused as the fluid flowed down and directly over my parted lips. I almost came from the gentle movement of the warm liquid as it trickled across the folds of my labia, channeled toward the junction where they joined together at my clit. I shuddered in pleasure at the feeling, even if it was only the subtlest of touch.

Jasmine suddenly interrupted my thoughts.

"Would you like to turn over now?"

It was the first time she had spoken directly to me since the massage started, and it surprised me in my catatonic, pre-orgasmic state. I practically flipped over like a fish out of water and spread my legs expectantly. Finally, I'd get some relief. Surely, she couldn't leave me hanging like this.

"It's time for your final grooming," she said. "I'll need you to part your legs a bit further to provide full access."

Grooming? I knew this was part of the process, but somehow it didn't seem fair to transition at this precise moment. At least I'd be able to stay on the comfortable massage table instead of the clinical vinyl chairs used by my regular esthetician.

Jasmine walked over to another cabinet by the makeup table and withdrew a leather bag from one of the drawers, then brought it back to the table. She reached into the bag and pulled out a cordless hair trimmer.

"Do you have a preference regarding your appearance?" she asked. "Do you prefer natural, neatly trimmed, or bare?"

I knew she was referring to my pubic hair, which I generally kept neatly trimmed. I'd always thought going fully bald was unnatural and unseemly, catering to men's prurient fantasies of fucking young schoolgirls. But in this situation, it seemed entirely appropriate, like I was stripping away all my camouflage and armor.

If tonight was all about being watched, I might as well bare myself in every sense of the word and truly let my inhibitions go. I began to fantasize about rubbing my bare pussy against Jasmine's while she poured warm oil between us. The more work she had to do on me, the more chance I'd have to make this last and hopefully get off.

I didn't hesitate. "Bare, thank you."

"As you wish," she said. "I'll remove the long hairs first with the trimmer, then shave you smooth with a razor."

No waxing? This was different. I was relieved to not have to bear the painful and violent trial of having my hairs ripped out en masse. Although shaving down there was always a scary proposition, I felt safe in the capable and practiced hands of this beautiful esthetician.

Jasmine nodded, then flipped a switch on the trimmer. The device buzzed softly as she placed it gently on my mound. I had only a light dusting of fur and it didn't take long for her to remove it with a few short strokes over my pubis. I shuddered as the vibrations penetrated deep into my core. If she had placed the flat head on my clitoris, I would have popped off in a millisecond. Instead, she turned the trimmer face-down and gently swiped the vibrating teeth against the sides of my vulva, sensuously separating my labia with her hands as she moved the device between my legs to trim the hairs on the inside and outside of my labia.

It was an insanely titillating feeling, but just clinical enough to bring me down from my plateau and shift my focus. My mind wandered to the upcoming feast, and I contemplated what surprises lay in wait at the main event. The hostesses had suggested there would be 'contact' of some sort during the meal, and I was intrigued exactly who and how it would be administered. The idea of being fully bald, cleansed, and thoroughly stimulated going into the event was an incredible rush.

Jasmine continued with the trimmer all the way down my perineum to my anus, barely touching me with the trimmer so as not to pinch any delicate tissues. Apparently there were no parts of my erogenous zone that would remain untouched, now—and perhaps later.

She turned off the trimmer and placed it at the foot of the table. Then she took a bottle of gel from the bag and spread the gel on her hands. Using both hands, she spread it gently between my legs, starting on my mound all the way down to my rosebud.

My body almost levitated above the table as Jasmine finally laid her hands directly on my clitoris. The gel had a mild stinging quality that added to the stimulating sensation. If this was meant to excite my follicles in preparation for the shave, it wasn't the only feature of my anatomy that it made erect. I could feel the hood of my clitoris retract as my button filled with blood and began to push outward. Suddenly, I was fully stimulated again and lusting for Jasmine's touch. I fantasized about her bending down and taking my swollen nub between her puffy lips and letting me come in her mouth.

Unfortunately, my satisfaction would have to wait a little longer. Instead, Jasmine reached into her bag and pulled out a straight-edge razor. In anyone else's hands, it might look threatening, especially in my prostrated and vulnerable position. But something about the way she delicately and sensuously opened the jackknifed tool instantly evaporated my fears. I could see how this type of razor would in fact give her better control safely cutting my stubs instead of the usual ladies plastic razor.

With her right hand, Jasmine gently laid the razor on its flat edge at the top of my mound, while she gently pulled my skin upwards with her other hand. Then she slowly turned the sharp edge perpendicular to my skin and began softly scraping the razor downwards. I could hear the bristling sound as the razor edge removed my nubs right down to the follicles. She repeated the pattern in one inch wide swipes on one side then the other of my pubis, being ever-so-careful to stop just where my clitoris lay quivering in a mixture of fear and excitement. There was something about the utter vulnerability of the procedure that made it the most erotic experience I'd ever had.

Jasmine used the same deft touch as she moved down my vulva and perineum, scraping the vestiges of stray hairs away with gentle swipes of the long blade, while sensuously separating my folds and flesh with her other hand. She took extra time and care around my anus and clit, using the gentlest and slowest motion I've ever felt someone apply to my body. The combination of fright and titillation as she probed my most sensitive body parts created a river of sensuous fluids running down my vulva. By this time, no shaving gel was necessary to provide a smooth gliding surface for the knife.

When she was finished, Jasmine retrieved a fresh wash towel from beside the sink and held it under the warm water faucet then twisted the excess water into the basin. She returned to the table and placed it over my splayed legs then gently cleansed the excess moisture and remaining shaving gel with gentle massaging movements of her hands. The warm, moist towel felt exquisite against my newly shaved skin. Jasmine's hands now felt comforting between my legs rather than erotic.

She had taken me on an incredibly sensuous erotic arc, right to the edge of ecstasy and back, to a quiet relaxed place. I exhaled fully and completely for the first time in almost an hour.

Jasmine removed the towel from between my legs and held up a large hand mirror at a forty-five degree angle toward me.

"What do you think?" she asked.

I tilted my head up and studied her masterpiece. Far from the usual red and swollen vulva that I typically experienced after the violent waxing with my regular esthetician, I'd never seen my pussy look so beautiful. Utterly bereft of any hair, my entire perineum from my pubic mound to my anus was totally bald, pink—and gorgeous. I just stared at my beautiful pussy, utterly transfixed by the transformation.

"You have to *feel* it to really appreciate how beautiful you are, Jade," Jasmine purred.

I moved my right hand down, running my fingers along the edges of my pussy. I gasped from a feeling I'd never felt before. It felt smooth as silk: no bumps or blemishes or cuts or bruises. It was almost as if I was feeling somebody else— somebody I'd never felt before. I couldn't stop my left hand joining the other in rubbing and caressing my sensitive organs.

Jasmine lowered the mirror and smiled at me as I felt the moisture begin to accumulate between my legs again.

"It's almost time for your dinner appointment," she said. "Why don't you save the best for last? I think you'll find plenty of ways to satisfy your appetite over the next couple of hours."

She lifted my kimono from the hook at the edge of the bathtub and held it open for me.

"I'll escort you downstairs now if you're ready. All you need to bring is your kimono and slippers—and your mask of course."

I sat up slowly and stepped off the massage table. Turning around, I held my arms out as Jasmine lifted one arm of the silk robe onto me then the other. Then she turned around to face me, wrapped the silk tie around me, and tied a single bow over my belly button. She retrieved my matching silk slippers and knelt down on one knee to gently lift my feet one at a time and place them softly inside. It took every ounce of my power not to grab her head and pull it into my pulsating pussy.

Jasmine stood up gracefully and smiled into my eyes.

"If you'll follow me, I'll escort you now to the fantasy feast."

She didn't bother putting her own robe on. Her tight little ass barely jiggled as she stepped smartly ahead of me. I wasn't sure if I'd have a chance to feel Jasmine's touch again before the evening was over, but for now I was in total bliss ogling her petite, curvaceous figure from behind...

Read More

ABOUT THE AUTHOR

If you would like to receive notification of new book(s) in Jade's Erotic Adventures, follow me at http://bookbub.com/authors/victoria-rush.

If you have a moment, please post a brief review on my Amazon book page at viewbook.at/peepshow . Even just a couple of sentences will help other readers find and enjoy this book as much as you hopefully did.

Follow, share, like, and comment at:

www.facebook.com/authorvictoriarush
www.pinterest.com/authorvictoriarush
www.twitter.com/authorvictoriarush
authorvictoriarush@outlook.com

Hope to see you again soon!